Dear Parent:
Your child's love of readin

D0580671

Every child learns to read in a different way and at his or her own speed. You can help your young reader improve and become more confident by encouraging his or her own interests and abilities. You can also guide your child's spiritual development by reading stories with biblical values and Bible stories, like I Can Read! books published by Zonderkidz. From books your child reads with you to the first books he or she reads alone, there are I Can Read! books for every stage of reading:

SHARED READING
Basic language, word repetition, and whimsical illustrations, ideal for sharing with your emergent reader.

BEGINNING READING
Short sentences, familiar words, and simple concepts for children eager to read on their own.

READING WITH HELP
Engaging stories, longer sentences, and language play for developing readers.

READING ALONE
Complex plots, challenging vocabulary, and high-interest topics for the independent reader.

ADVANCED READING
Short paragraphs, chapters, and exciting themes for the perfect bridge to chapter books.

I Can Read! books have introduced children to the joy of reading since 1957. Featuring award-winning authors and illustrators and a fabulous cast of beloved characters, I Can Read! books set the standard for beginning readers.

A lifetime of discovery begins with the magical words "I (

AR Level 1.9

AR Points 0.5

Q2#165315

Visit www.icanread.com for information on enriching your child's rea
Visit www.zonderkidz.com for more Zonderkidz I Can Read

Anyone who hides his sins doesn't succeed.
But anyone who admits his sins
and gives them up finds mercy.
— Proverbs 28:13 NIrV

ZONDERKIDZ

Bob and Larry in The Case of the Messy Sleepover
©2013 Big Idea Entertainment, LLC. VEGGIETALES®, character names, likenesses
and other indicia are trademarks of and copyrighted by Big Idea Entertainment, LLC.
All rights reserved.
Illustrations ©2011 by Big Idea Entertainment, Inc.

Requests for information should be addressed to:

Zonderkidz, 5300 Patterson Ave SE, Grand Rapids, Michigan 49530

ISBN 978-0-310-74166-4

Editor: Mary Hassinger
Art direction: Karen Poth
Cover design: Karen Poth
Interior design: Ron Eddy

Printed in China

I Can Read!

Bob and Larry in The Case of the Messy Sleepover

story by Karen Poth

My name is Detective Larry.

This is my partner, Bob.

We solve mysteries.

Sometimes our jobs
are very messy.
Here is one of our
stories.

RING, RING!
The phone rang early
in the morning.

It was Madame Blueberry.

She was babysitting.

And she had a big mess.

We went to Madame Blueberry's house.

"Good morning," I said.

I introduced my stuffed badger.

"Why did you bring that?"
Bob asked.

"You have a badge," I said.

"So, I brought my badger."

Madame Blueberry told her story.
"Percy Pea and his friends
spent the night last night," she said.

"This morning their room is a mess,"
she said. "No one will help me
clean it up!"

We went upstairs.
Pancakes, clothes, and syrup
were all over the floor.

The boys were on the bed.

They were watching TV.

Lenny Carrot was sitting alone.

He looked sad.

"Do you know who
made this mess?"
Bob asked.
No one said a thing.
I made a note of that.

Suddenly Lenny spoke.

"Percy made the mess," he said.

"He spilled syrup
and threw clothes all over."

"Wait a minute," Percy said.

"I didn't make this mess.

"Harold and Joe did it.

They had a pillow fight,"

Percy said. "They made the mess."

"I didn't," Harold said.

"Lenny and Percy did it."

"No, LENNY and HAROLD did it,"
Joe said.

Suddenly Joe hit

Harold with a pillow.

Then Lenny threw a pillow at Percy.

Soon the boys were fighting.

The mess was getting bigger.

Percy squirted syrup at Lenny!

Harold squirted Joe!

The pillows broke open.

Feathers flew everywhere.

It was BAD!

"Stop it," Bob said.

"God wants us to be helpful."

They were not being helpful.

They were not
even being nice.

Then it happened.

"I'm sorry," Harold said.

"I'm sorry too," Percy said.

"I forgive you,"
said Madame Blueberry.
"Let's clean it up together."

Once the room was clean,
we had to clean the boys.

We all went outside

and played in the sprinkler.

It was the perfect way to clean up!

Everyone played all day.

Even my badger had fun!